TURTLE SPRING

Deborah Turney Zagwÿn

Tricycle Press
Berkeley, California

For Leo

Tricycle Press (a little division of Ten Speed Press)
P.O. Box 7123, Berkeley, California 94707
www.tenspeed.com
Book design by Tasha Hall

The Library of Congress has catalogued an earlier edition as follows:
Zagwÿn, Deborah Turney.
    Turtle spring / Deborah Turney Zagwÿn.
        p.   cm.
    Summary: The changing seasons bring surprises to
Clee, including a new baby brother early in the year and
a turtle whose life seems to crawl away in the winter.
    ISBN 1-883672-53-8
    [1. Seasons—Fiction. 2. Brothers and sisters—Fiction.
3. Turtles—Fiction.]   I. Title.
PZ7.Z245Tu   1997   97-15608
[E]—dc21   CIP
                                                       AC

First Tricycle Press printing, 1998
First paperback printing, 2001
ISBN 1-883672-53-8 (hardcover)
ISBN 1-58246-052-3 (paperback)
Printed in Singapore
1 2 3 4 5 6 7— 05 04 03 02 01

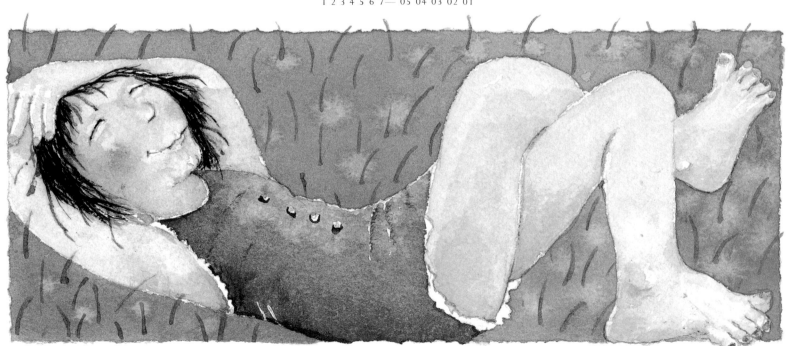

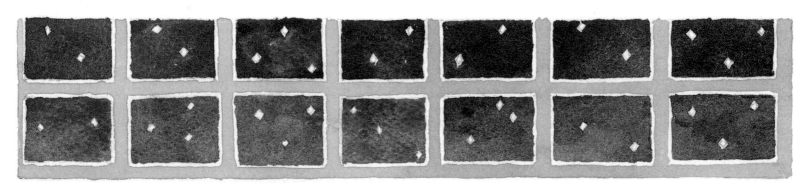

She will find a place,
draw her life deep within herself
and wait out the coming and
going of the ice.
—David M. Carroll, THE YEAR OF THE TURTLE

*F*or Clee it was a summer of hellos and goodbyes.
    Clee's relatives came. Clee's relatives went. But her
new red-faced baby brother stayed for good.

"*A*ren't you the lucky one?" everyone insisted from orbits around the crib. Clee felt like a lost moon.

One visitor, Uncle Fishtank Hal, knew all about lost moons. Clee's family called him Fishtank because he lived on a barge with aquariums for windows.

"I have brought something for Clee," he boomed. "She's bungeed to my bike and she ain't happy about the trip!"

Then Fishtank Hal whispered
in Clee's ear, "She's a rebel
with no cause, jumped tank
one time too many. She ain't
a gift for a baby. She's too big
and would only pinch it." Clee
knew the feeling.

*I*t was late summer when Clee's father said goodbye. Uncle Fishtank Hal was ferrying him to an island off the coast.

"It's a big job," Clee's father told her ruefully. "I won't be finished for months."

*S*eptember was quiet without the sound of Clee's father whistling in the garden. There were no hammering-on-the-porch or firewood-thumping-in-the-woodshed sounds. The apples ripened, without him.

In the sandbox Clee's turtle sunned herself. She looked contented, having just gobbled three worms. Her split pea eyes were smiley slits.

*T*he autumn sun lasted until mid-October and then the wind blew it away. Sometimes Clee worried that the turtle had escaped but then found her under a roof of leaves, having a nap.

"You should consider bringing her in at night," Clee's mother advised. "It's getting colder—too cold for a southern breed of turtle."

*I*n November the house was full of baby.

"Afternoon's his crabby time, Clee." Her mother's braid stuck out over one ear.

One morning Clee dreamed that she had forgotten something.

The feeling tugged her awake and pulled her outside to the sandbox. The ground was crunchy under Clee's feet and the sand was hard and cold to the touch. Her turtle was missing. The shabby leaves offered no shelter now.

"Why didn't I take her inside? Why didn't I take her inside?" Clee's teeth chattered.

Clee examined the frost at her feet. No clues. No turtle. Looking closer, she noticed traces of scrambling and clawing in one corner. There, brittle leaves and sticks had formed a frozen ramp. Her turtle had escaped over this and under the garden fence. The tracks in the frost ended at the compost pile.

*T*hat's where Clee found her, beneath a layer of grass clippings and rotting leaves. In an effort to stay warm, the turtle had pulled her feet and head into the heart of her shell. Now she was stone still, stone cold.

*L*ater, Clee told her mother about burying the turtle in the compost heap. "I made the hole deep so the coyotes wouldn't dig it up."

Her mother held her close and smoothed her hair. "Sometimes even carrying a house on your back can't keep you safe when you're a southern breed of turtle," Clee's mother said gently. "The northern seasons slip one into the other and weather can bring both good and bad surprises."

*D*ecember brought bitter weather. Clee's father's voice crackled over the radio telephone.

"Work's dragging on. Wind's fierce. I'm marooned!" the receiver spat out.

A pile of snow grew between the sandbox and the garden compost. Clee imagined her turtle, curled up and frozen beneath it.

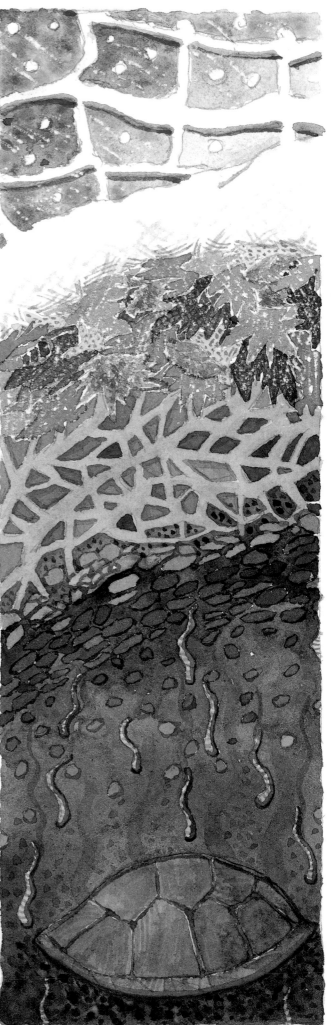

The storms continued.

"There has never been a winter," gloated the radio weatherman, "like this one." Clee's house grew a shell of snow. Inside, only her brother was lively—rolling, sitting, crawling, and sucking on everything in sight. He loved the warm kitchen best.

*T*he January sun dawned bright and cold. Clee scratched pictures
for her brother in the window frost. She showed him how to
breathe holes in the lace patterns.

*T*he countryside was paper white. Winter games were written with mittens and boots on a pad of snow—snow angels, snow forts, snow trails, snowballs, snowmen. Clee sat her little brother in a baking pan and twirled him until he was silly, giggling, dizzy. Beyond the snowbank was the sandbox and, beyond that, the compost mound.

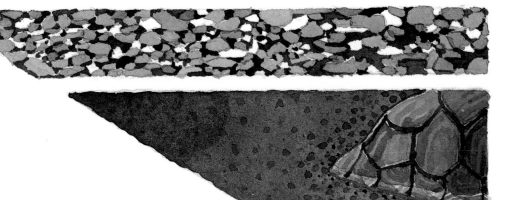

Clee never made trails for her brother in that direction.

In late February the snow changed. It became gritty, like frozen sand.

"Old snow," sighed Clee's mother.

"Sugar snow," wrote Clee's father.

*O*ver and over it melted, refreezing into an icy crust. In early March Clee could walk on it. Sometimes flakes of snow fell but the afternoon sun winked them away. The winds blew lukewarm and playful from the south.

"Spring melt!" sang Clee's mother.

"Job's done!" wrote Clee's father. "Be home soon."

By early April the big snowbanks were disappearing. The garden emerged shabby and moist. In the mornings steam from the compost heap wafted over the sandbox.

"Like it was cooking," Clee thought sourly.

A week later Clee noticed the flowers in the corners of her sandbox.

"Crocuses and snowdrops," her mother smiled. "Messengers of spring!"

Clee carried her squirming brother onto the porch for a closer look.

The sharp sweet smell of old and new growth drew them to the garden's edge. Clee set him down in a corner of the sandbox.

Yes, there were flowers growing out of the sand, and green-tipped grass shoots, too. Clee squatted next to her brother and tried not to look at the compost pile. But she could see it out of the corner of her eye and, worse than that, little gusts of wind were lifting the leaves. There was movement. Clee bit her lip to stop the tears.

Clee's little brother saw it first. A patchwork creature was inching its way down the compost slope.

The boy fell back into the wet sand laughing. He was thrilled to have found a creature who crawled slower than he did!

*A*s for Clee, she could not believe her eyes. Her turtle was very much alive and always had been. It was heading towards the sandbox with a surefooted stubbornness that Uncle Fishtank Hal knew well…a rebel with no cause, jumped tank one time too many! The northern seasons had slipped one into the other but her southern breed of turtle had its own calendar, knowing when to tunnel and sleep and when to wake up. It was the best surprise.

"Kee!" Her little brother chuckled and
poured sand down her boot.

In the wild, Red-eared Slider turtles like Clee's live in the southeastern United States. When the weather turns cold, many turtles hibernate, which means they stop eating and they burrow underground for a long winter's nap. They may look dead, but the warmth of spring wakes them up from their deep, deep sleep.

A compost heap is a mixture of yard clippings, leaves, and kitchen vegetable parings, layered and rotting nicely. The compost heap makes a good shelter for the turtle's winter hibernation because it is warm.